The Airship®

''Dedicated to Wendy''
This story tells the value of having
a dream to follow.

Story by:
Ken Forsse

Illustrated by:
David High
Russell Hicks
Valerie Edwards
Rennie Rau

Grubby® Newton Gimmick® Princess Aruzia™ Prince Arin™ Leota™ Wooly What's–It® Fobs™

Teddy

Hi! My name is Teddy Ruxpin. Can you and I be friends? I really enjoy talking to people. I would like you to meet some of my other friends, too. We're going to have lots of good times together. Now, listen to this sound . . .

That sound reminds you to open the book to page one. Each time you hear that sound again, you turn a page. Okay? There's a picture of Grubby. He's been a good friend of mine for a long time. Say hello to our new friend, Grubby.

Grubby

Oh, hi there. How are you? Hummm.

Teddy

Remember . . . Turn the page.

Teddy
Hey Grubby, do you remember this song?

Grubby
Yeah, I sure do.

Friends are people that you help
When they have things to do.
Friends are there to lend a hand
When there are things that you must do.

That's what friends are for . . .

"My Friend"
Your friend, your friend
Is what I'd like to be.
Your friend, your friend
'Cause I like you.
Do you like me?

My friend, my friend
I'd like for you to be.
My friend, my friend,
I'm nice to you,
You're nice to me.

Friendship is a lovely word.
It makes a lovely sound.
Friends are people that you like
And like to be around . . .

Your friend, your friend
Is what I'd like to be.
Your friend, your friend
'Cause I like you.
Do you like me?

Of course, Grubby . . .

My friend, my friend
I'd like for you to be.
My friend, that's you, my friend,
I'm nice to you,
You're nice to me.

Your friend, your friend
Your friend, your friend
Is what I'd like to be.
Your friend, your friend
Your friend, your friend
'Cause I like you.
Do you like me?

My friend, my friend
My friend, my friend
I'd like for you to be.
My friend, my friend,
My friend, my friend,
I'm nice to you.
You're nice to me.

Friends can make you smile when you
Are sort of feeling sad.
And friends will make you happy
And I'm real glad I have you for
My friend, my friend, my friend.

Teddy

Grubby and I had always wanted to go in search of new and wonderful things. Then one day we found an old treasure map. The treasure was supposed to be hidden in the far-off land of Grundo. And so we left our homeland of Rillonia and set out on our great adventure.

HARD TO FIND CITY

GRUNDO

Teddy

Let's go to far-off places
And search for treasures bright.

Grundo was a long way from Rillonia and after walking for many days, it didn't seem like we had made much progress.

Grubby

Teddy, my feet are getting sore. I must have stepped on every rock between Rillonia and here. You didn't tell me that adventure seeking would be this hard on my feet.

Teddy

As you can see, Grubby does have a lot of feet to worry about. So we decided to camp there overnight. The next morning Grubby's feet were better and we continued on our journey. That was the day we met Newton Gimmick!

Gimmick

Oh, hello there, hee-hee. My name is Newton Gimmick, but everyone just calls me Gimmick. Hee-hee, I'm an inventor.

Teddy

Oh yes, indeed. We discovered that Gimmick is a marvelous inventor.

Gimmick

Oh, I think "marvelous" inventor might be exaggerating. It would probably be sufficient to say "wonderful" inventor.

Grubby

We also discovered that Gimmick is modest.

Teddy

We told Gimmick that we were on a journey to find a treasure. He said that one of his latest inventions might be very useful to us. Grubby and I were very interested, so we went to Gimmick's house to see just what this new invention was.

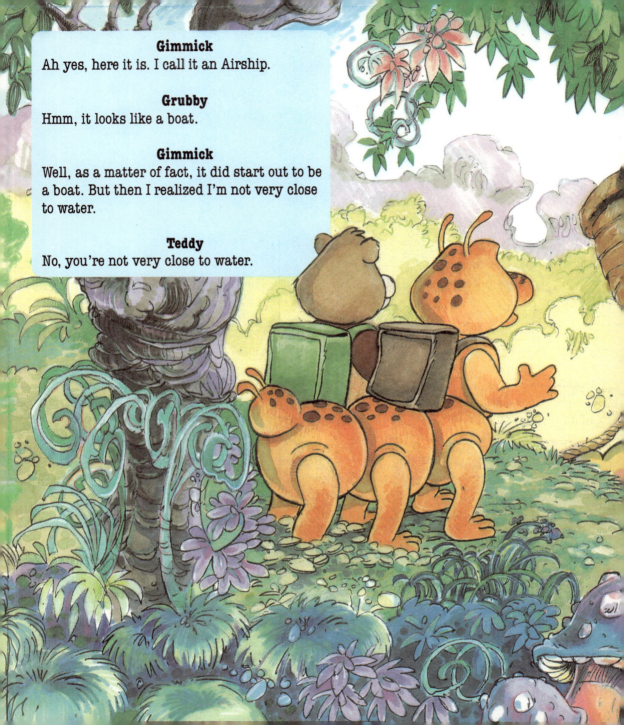

Gimmick
Ah yes, here it is. I call it an Airship.

Grubby
Hmm, it looks like a boat.

Gimmick
Well, as a matter of fact, it did start out to be a boat. But then I realized I'm not very close to water.

Teddy
No, you're not very close to water.

Grubby
Yeah, it would be kinda good for a boat to be close to water.

Gimmick
Precisely! That was my exact conclusion, but then the idea hit me. If a boat could float on water, it could also float on air—if the air is hot, that is.

Teddy
Gimmick explained that by pumping hot air into a giant air bag under the ship, the hot air would rise and cause the ship to lift off the ground. It sounded logical, but somehow something didn't seem quite right.

Grubby
Teddy, uh, something doesn't seem quite right.

Teddy
As the air bag filled with hot air, the ship began to lift off the ground.

Grubby
Hey Teddy, it's working!

Gimmick
Ah yes, just as I expected. Make sure all the tether lines are tight. Everyone get aboard!

Teddy

The ship lifted off the ground, and Newton Gimmick was delighted with his new invention . . . but somehow something still didn't seem quite right. Do you know what it was?

Grubby

Teddy, something still doesn't seem quite right. And I think I know what it is! Ohhh!!!

Teddy

Hey! We're tipping over! Watch out, Grubby! Ohhh!!!

Teddy
The Airship had turned upside down and crashed.

Gimmick
Hmm . . . apparently something wasn't quite right.

Grubby
Oh really? Maybe it was the hot air bag
trying to get out from under the ship.

Gimmick
Hmm . . . yes, Grubby. That may be it.

Teddy

What Grubby said was correct. By any chance, did you expect what would happen? We discovered that the hot air should pull the ship up into the sky, not push it, which meant the ship would have to be suspended by ropes from the air bag.

Gimmick

Indeed, Teddy. And once we had done that, everything was alright.

Teddy

Well, almost alright anyway. You see, we could make the ship go up and down okay, but we couldn't steer it very well. In fact, we got stuck in a tree. Suddenly, we heard a tiny voice.

Leota

Just what are you doing in my tree?

Gimmick

Huh? Who said that?

Leota

I said that! And I'll say it again. Just what are you doing in my tree?

Teddy

We discovered that the voice was coming from – a tiny flying lady!

Grubby

Hey, would ya look at that! What is it?

Leota

I'm a Woodsprite.

Gimmick

No, there is no such thing as a Woodsprite.

Leota

Oh no! And I suppose there's no such thing as a big bag of air stuck in my tree. But there it is, big as life!

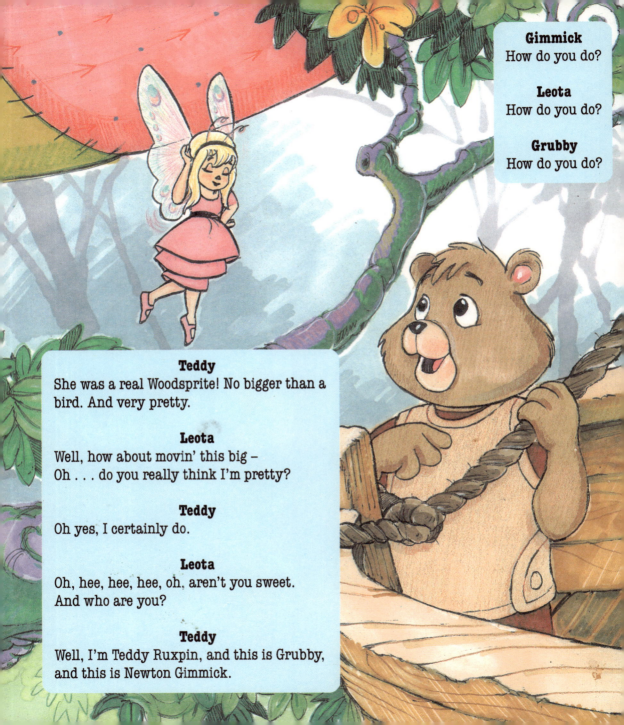

Gimmick
How do you do?

Leota
How do you do?

Grubby
How do you do?

Teddy
She was a real Woodsprite! No bigger than a bird. And very pretty.

Leota
Well, how about movin' this big –
Oh . . . do you really think I'm pretty?

Teddy
Oh yes, I certainly do.

Leota
Oh, hee, hee, hee, oh, aren't you sweet. And who are you?

Teddy
Well, I'm Teddy Ruxpin, and this is Grubby, and this is Newton Gimmick.

Teddy

Leota showed us how to get down out of the
tree. Then she gave us some ideas about
steering the Airship.

Leota

Now, in order for your Airship to move in any
given direction, you must apply a force in the
opposite direction, such as this large manu-
ally driven propeller. Then you will have to
know something about the effect of wind and
various aspects of navigation. It's very
simple.

Teddy

Well, it all sounded very confusing at first,
but Leota had been flying all of her life and
knew just what we should do to make the
Airship work.

Teddy

And we were off on our way to Grundo . . . in search of adventure and maybe to find a treasure. Grubby and I had met two new friends, Newton Gimmick and Leota the Woodsprite. And I think we started to learn that it probably wouldn't matter too much if we ever found the treasure or not. The important thing would be the people we would meet and the things we would discover along the way.

"Come and Discover"

Come and discover the world with me.
There are lots of people we can meet
Lots of things to see.

So come and discover the world with me.
Oh boy . . . Like what makes
The leaves in Autumn fall?
What irritates a honeybee?

Why are some people six feet tall
And others only three?
What makes the snow in winter fall?
How does a sheep dog see?

How come my favorite rubber ball
Can bounce into a tree?
And sometimes when I trip and fall,
Why does the ground jump up at me?
Huh–I never thought about that.

Come and discover the world with me.
There are lots of people we can meet
Lots of things to see.

Teddy

And so, at last the Airship flew perfectly. We said goodbye to Leota . . .

Leota

Goodbye . . . goodbye.

Grubby & Gimmick

Goodbye . . . toodle – ooooo, goodbye.

So come and discover the world with me.
Do you think that a snowflake knows
Just what shape it's going to be?

Now do you think a duck has toes?
Why does a dog have fleas?
Why are there freckles on my nose?
What causes me to sneeze?
Where does a balloon go
When you set it free?
And overnight a mushroom grows.
But it takes years to grow a tree.
Huh. Don't ask me . . . o.k.

Come and discover the world with me.
There are lots of people we can meet
Lots of things to see.

So come and discover the
World with me.
Come on Teddy . . . let's go!
It's a world full of wonders
And it's here for you and me.

Come and discover the
World with me.
My friend, my friend.
Come and discover
The world with me.
My friend, my friend.
Come and discover
The world . . .
My friend, my friend.